The Magic Bed

John Burningham

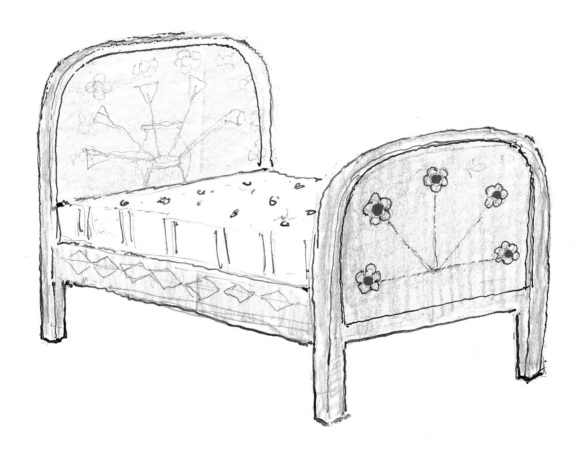

Jonathan Cape
London

To Harriet

THE MAGIC BED
A Jonathan Cape Book: 0 224 06468 1

Published in Great Britain by Jonathan Cape,
an imprint of Random House Children's Books

This edition published 2003

1 3 5 7 9 10 8 6 4 2

Copyright © John Burningham, 2003

The right of John Burningham to be identified as the author
of this work has been asserted in accordance with the Copyright,
Designs and Patents Act 1988.

RANDOM HOUSE CHILDREN'S BOOKS
61–63 Uxbridge Road, London W5 5SA
A division of The Random House Group Ltd.

RANDOM HOUSE AUSTRALIA (PTY) LTD
20 Alfred Street, Milsons Point, Sydney,
New South Wales 2061, Australia

RANDOM HOUSE NEW ZEALAND LTD
18 Poland Road, Glenfield, Auckland 10, New Zealand

RANDOM HOUSE (PTY) LTD
Endulini, 5A Jubilee Road, Parktown 2193, South Africa

THE RANDOM HOUSE GROUP Limited Reg. No. 954009
www.kidsatrandomhouse.co.uk

A CIP catalogue record for this book is available from the British Library

Printed in Malaysia by Tien Wah Press [PTE] Ltd

'That bed is far too small for you now, Georgie.
Why don't you and Frank go down to the shopping
centre to buy a new one?'

On the way to the shopping centre, Georgie saw
a shop that sold old furniture.
'Look, Frank,' said Georgie. 'Maybe they'll have
a bed in there.'

They parked the car and went inside.

'Do you have a bed that would be right
for this boy?' said Frank.
'Beds . . . beds . . . yes, I do have a little
old bed somewhere,' said the man.

After some time, the man found the bed.
'The lady this bed came from
said it was magic,' he said,
'and that you could travel in it.'

Frank and Georgie bought the bed.
They tied the bed to the top of the car and took it home.

Georgie and Frank cleaned the bed all over.

'Look, Georgie,' said Frank, 'there's some writing here. It's very faint.'

'What does it say?' said Georgie.

'It says: "In this bed you will travel far.

First say your prayers and then say . . ."

I can't read the last word. It says M, something, something, something, Y.'

'What on earth have you got there?' said Georgie's granny.
'Why did you get that awful old bed? Why didn't you go
to the shopping centre and buy a new one?'
'It's a lovely bed,' said Georgie, 'and it's magic. You can travel in it.'

That evening, Georgie got ready for bed early.

He said his prayers and then tried to say the magic word.
He tried: *money, matey, mummy, murky, molly, mandy,*
milly, messy, minty, mousy . . .
But nothing happened and Georgie went to sleep.

'How did you get on last night in your magic bed?
Did you go to the moon or up the Amazon?'

That night Georgie went to bed early again and tried to guess the magic word. He must have got it right because suddenly . . .

he was travelling way over the city.

Georgie's bed landed in a field.
Lots of gnomes and fairies
arrived and he read them
a bedtime story.

At breakfast the next day, Georgie
decided not to tell anyone about
where he had been during the night.

That evening Georgie was off again.
This time he was travelling over the jungle.

Georgie came across a young tiger that was lost.
It had wandered away from its parents and didn't
know how to get back home.

He took the young tiger back to its
mother and father, who were very pleased
that Georgie had found their child.

On one of his journeys, Georgie found
a chest full of treasure in a cave.

But there were some pirates who were very
angry because they thought the treasure was theirs.

They chased Georgie down the beach . . .

and he only just managed to escape.

Some nights, Georgie would go for a swim with the dolphins, which is why his bed was sometimes wet in the mornings.

Another night, Georgie gave a lift to some geese
that were very tired because they had flown a long way.
Then he had a race with some witches.

Then came the day when they went away on their holidays.
They waved goodbye to Georgie's granny and set off.

While they were away, Georgie forgot all about his magic bed.

The holiday soon ended,
and they all came home.

'There is a lovely present for you, Georgie.
It's in your room,' said his granny.

Georgie rushed up to his room and there in the corner
was a brand new bed.
'What have you done with my magic bed?' said Georgie.
'Oh, that nasty old bed went down to the dump today,'
said Granny.

Georgie raced out of the house, down the steps
and along the road to the dump.

He just managed to get through the gates as the dump was closing.
There, on top of a rubbish skip, was Georgie's magic bed.

Georgie climbed up into the skip. He leaped onto his bed,
said the magic word, and the bed rose quickly into the sky.

Now if you lie very still in your bed and find *your* magic word, perhaps you could travel far away like Georgie.